Shakespeare Scenes

Monologues for young female actors

Kim Gilbert

Shakespeare Scenes

Copyright © 2020 Kim Gilbert

All rights reserved.

ISBN: 9798634856179

DEDICATION

This collection of Shakespearean scenes, is dedicated to all students of drama and those readers with a love of the greatest writer to have ever lived – William Shakespeare. Continue to explore his works. I hope you gain as much satisfaction from them as I have.

Shakespeare Scenes

ACKNOWLEDGEMENTS

A special thanks goes to my husband, Steve who has prepared this book for publication. He has bailed me out on numerous occasions over the years with his technical expertise.

TABLE OF CONTENTS

Introduction

About William Shakespeare

Shakespeare's Writing Style

A Midsummer Night's Dream	1
As You Like It	27
The Tempest	37
Twelfth Night	49
The Two Gentlemen of Verona	63
The Merchant of Venice	73
Hamlet	81
Cymbeline	89
Henry VI (Part 1)	93
King Lear	97
Macbeth	101
Romeo & Juliet	107

Shakespeare Scenes

INTRODUCTION

I have compiled and edited this collection of Shakespearean monologue scenes for young female actors to study as well as enjoy. These scenes are suitable for a range of acting exams and awards as well as for auditions and festivals. I have tried and tested these scenes with numerous students over the years with great success and more importantly, they have thoroughly enjoyed working on them. I believe, it is crucial to choose characters within ones' playing range. This collection contains only suitable characters for young teenage actors to play. The older Shakespearean characters have been omitted. From my experience, I have seen many young actors tackling characters which are often unsuited to their age range and ability. There will be plenty of time in the future to tackle the more mature and demanding female characters which Shakespeare so brilliantly creates. Learn to build your skills and technique systematically with the younger, wonderfully written characters first before you attempt to move forwards to the demands of the older Shakespearean characters.

The monologues in this collection are taken from a range of comic and tragic plays: A Midsummer Night's Dream, The Tempest, Twelfth Night, The Two Gentlemen of Verona, The Merchant of Venice, Romeo & Juliet, Hamlet, Cymbeline, Macbeth, Henry VI and King Lear. There is a biography on Shakespeare, some notes about his writing style and a short synopsis of each play. Each scene has an introduction prepared suitable for exam or festival work and are also timed with exams and festival work in mind. I hope you enjoy this collection.

Shakespeare Scenes

WILLIAM SHAKESPEARE 1564-1616

Shakespeare was born in Stratford-on-Avon. It is thought that he went to the Grammar School even though there are no records to prove this. His parents were both illiterate. William certainly went on to make a name for himself and the surname of Shakespeare, despite being quite common in those days, became famous. William Shakespeare's legacy was his 37 world renowned plays as well as his 154 sonnets

Shakespeare married Anne Hathaway, she was 8yrs older than William; the couple had 3 children by the time he was 21, Susanna and twins Judith and Hamnet. Shakespeare finally left Stratford for London to seek his fortune, possibly at the age of around 23yrs. It is thought that the 'Queen's Men' visited Stratford to perform and William joined them as a young recruit. Shakespeare's first London patron was James Burbage, a leading theatrical manager of the time. Later, his son Richard Burbage would play many of Shakespeare's leading roles. Many of the leading playwrights of the day were jealous of Shakespeare and they mocked him for not having been to University. By the age of twenty-eight, Shakespeare was well established in London as an actor and playwright. Richard Burbage later formed a new troupe called the Lord Chamberlain's Men, of which Shakespeare was a member and remained so until the end of his career. Burbage's carpenters built the highly successful Globe Theatre in 1599 with a capacity of 2,500- 3,000. The original Globe Theatre in London was known as 'The Wooden 'O' because of its shape.
Shakespeare owned a tenth of this theatre. Shakespeare wrote a range of plays loosely categorised as tragedies, comedies and histories. Shakespeare based the plots of his plays on traditional stories, often changing them slightly or adding music and songs to make them more interesting. Superstition was as important as religion in Elizabethan times. That is why so many of Shakespeare's plays feature ghosts, witches, spells, magic, fairies and storms and shipwrecks.

It certainly helped that Queen Elizabeth 1 loved the theatre and invited players to entertain at Court. There were no female actresses, only male actors. The young boys played the women's parts. Many of the audience had to stand to watch the plays and were known as groundlings. There were, of course, seats and shelter available at a higher price for the wealthier. If an Elizabethan audience didn't like a play, they often booed and jeered, cracked nuts and threw orange skins.

The actors were given only their own parts to the play. It wasn't until the 16th and 17th Century that printing became available, enabling Shakespeare's plays to be published. However, printers would often change the words of a playwrights play in order for them to fit onto the page!

Unfortunately, it was due to The Great Plague in 1665 that all London theatres were closed down, forcing players to tour the rest of the country.

Shakespeare's characters and plots

Shakespeare's characters are depicted as real people with 'universal' emotions. His variety of characters interrelate with other characters creating great interest within the plot. His comedies often include stock-characters, which are easily recognizable characters with common features and characteristics.

Acting a Shakespearean Character

When preparing for acting a role one should always study the play as a whole and approach the scene in context with the whole play.

Here are some questions to consider.

Is your character a central character (i.e. the hero or heroine) providing strength and leadership. Perhaps your character is a stock character providing comedy or light relief to the plot?

What are your character's likes, dislikes?

Map your character's journey throughout the play?

How does your character develop throughout the play?

What is your character's role/purpose in the play? Try to establish their objective.

Does this character suit your acting skills and personality?

What does your character look like? Think about how you might like to play your character in terms of physical and vocal skills?

What characteristics would the actor need to play this character?

How do you relate to your character? Do you like your character?

How do you envisage your character in costume?

<u>Shakespeare's Writing style</u>

<u>Metre and Rhythm</u>

English is a stress language. This means that our language is made up of strong and weak stresses. Verse is made of these stresses into regular patterns which is what we call METRE.

A metrical unit is called a FOOT. This comes from ancient Greece, where, in dance, the foot was raised up and down on the beat of a bar of music.

A metrical line is named according to the number of feet in a line.

AN IAMBIC FOOT

An Iambic foot has one unstressed & one stressed syllable OR one weak syllable & one strong syllable.

Iambic Pentametre (used by Shakespeare & other writers) is made up of 5 feet of iambic rhythms. e.g. de **dum**/de **dum**/de **dum**/de **dum**/de **dum**. e.g. 'The **clock** struck **nine** when **I** did **send** the **nurse**' (from Romeo & Juliet) and 'I **left** no **ring** with **her**, what **means** this **lady**?' (from Twelfth Night).

The rhythm resembles the beating of the human heart and is closest to natural rhythms of natural speech. Blank verse is verse without rhyme and is therefore more natural in sound and ideal for play writing.

Shakespeare wrote his plays in iambic pentametre. He uses blank verse (verse without rhyme). It has no regular rhyme and is therefore ideal for writing verse plays. There are, however, inversions and other variations which are added to create variety in the rhythm. Be aware of the hemistich: where one character speaks half a line and the next character finishes it. This is where you see split lines on a page between characters speaking.

Shakespeare's Language

Here are some of Shakespeare's famous expressions which we still use today.

Shakespeare's plays were full of insults and rude words. Some of these words were highly insulting and seem very amusing to present day audiences. Here are some examples …

There's method in my madness: The world's your oyster: Love is blind: beetle-head: pottle-deep: pribbling: flap-mouthed: fat-kidneyed: wart-necked: swag-bellied: onion-eyed: bum-bailey: maggot-pie: pignut. To name but a few!

Shakespeare Scenes

The Scenes

Shakespeare Scenes

A MIDSUMMER NIGHT'S DREAM

A Midsummer Night's Dream is a magical play, most of which takes place in a forest outside of Athens. The play opens in Theseus's court, in Athens. Egeus, Hermia's father is demanding that Hermia marries a young man named Demetrius. However, Hermia is in love with Lysander. This is where the trouble begins! Helena, meanwhile, loves Demetrius and when she learns that Hermia and Lysander are planning to run away together, Helena uses this opportunity to inform Demetrius, hoping that his affections will turn towards her.

From this point onwards, the play is set in the forest. It is midsummer's night, the only time when spirits and mortals are able to see each other. The spirit world spies on the human world and when Oberon spots Demetrius treating Helena badly, he decides to resolve this by sending his spirit Puck, to squeeze a magical love juice into Demetrius's eyes to force him to fall in love with her. However, the mischievous Puck, mistakenly squeezes the love juice into Lysander's eyes and so Lysander consequently falls in love with Helena. This all takes place in the middle of the play and results in a hilarious quarrel between the four lovers. Helena now has two men in love with her and poor Hermia is left very confused.

There is also a sub-plot which involves a group of Athenian workers who are rehearsing a play for the Duke of Athen's wedding. Their play rehearsals are extremely amusing and Bottom falls prey to the love juice too and, much to everyone's amusement, ends up being seduced by the Queen of the fairies, Titania.

As in all comedies, there is a happy ending. The play is selected to be performed at the wedding party of Theseus and Hippolyta. The four lovers are reunited with each other i.e Hermia and Lysander are married alongside Helena and Demetrius and all troubles in the forest are quickly forgotten. After all, it was merely a dream!

Shakespeare Scenes

Shakespeare Scenes

A MIDSUMMER NIGHT'S DREAM ACT 1, SC 1

(*Helena has just learned that Hermia and Lysander are planning to run away with each other, and is feeling very sorry for herself*)

Helena:

How happy some o'er other some can be!

Through Athens I am thought as fair as she.

But what of that? Demetrius thinks not so;

He will not know what all but he do know:

And as he errs, doting on Hermia's eyes,

So I, admiring of his qualities.

Things base and vile, holding no quantity,

Love can transpose to form and dignity.

Love looks not with the eyes, but with the mind,

And therefore is winged Cupid painted blind.

Nor hath Love's mind of any judgement taste;

Wings and no eyes figure unheedy haste:

And therefore is Love said to be a child,

Because in choice he is so oft beguiled.

As waggish boys in fame themselves forswear;

So the boy Love is perjured everywhere;

For ere Demetrius looked on Hermia's eyne,

He hailed down oaths that he was only mine;

And when this hail some heat from Hermia felt,

So he dissolved, and showers of oaths did melt.

I will go tell him of fair Hermia's flight;

Then to the wood will he tomorrow night

Pursue her; and for this intelligence,

If I have thanks, it is a dear expense.

But herein mean I to enrich my pain,

To have his sight thither, and back again.

A MIDSUMMER NIGHT'S DREAM ACT 2, SC 1

(Demetrius enters, closely followed by Helena expressing her love for him)

Helena:

You draw me, you hard-hearted adamant,

But yet you draw not iron, for my heart

Is true as steel. Leave you your power to draw,

And I shall have no power to follow you.

I am your spaniel; and, Demetrius,

The more you beat me, I will fawn on you.

Use me but as your spaniel; spurn me, strike me,

Neglect me, lose me; only give me leave,

Unworthy as I am, to follow you.

What worser place can I beg in your love,

And yet a place of high respect with me,

Than to be used as you use your dog?

Your virtue is my privilege: for that

It is not night when I do see your face,

Therefore, I think I am not in the night;

Nor doth this wood lack worlds of company,

For you, in my respect, are all the world.

Then how can it be said I am alone,

When all the world is here to look on me?

The wildest hath not such a heart as you.

Run when you will, the story shall be changed:

Apollo flies, and Daphne holds the chase;

The dove pursues the griffin, the mild hind

Makes speed to catch the tiger; bootless speed,

When cowardice pursues, and valour flies.

Ay, in the temple, in the town, the field

You do me mischief. Fie, Demetrius;

Your wrongs do set a scandal on my sex:

We cannot fight for love, as men may do;

We should be wooed, and were not made to woo.

I'll follow thee, and make a heaven of hell,

To die upon the hand I love so well.

A MIDSUMMER NIGHT'S DREAM ACT 2, SC 2

(Helena does not understand why Lysander is suddenly in love with her).

Helena:

O, I am out of breath in this fond chase.

The more my prayer, the lesser is my grace.

Happy is Hermia, wheresoever she lies;

For she hath blessed and attractive eyes.

How came her eyes so bright? Not with salt tears:

If so, my eyes are oftener wash'd than hers.

No, no, I am as ugly as a bear;

For beasts that meet me run away for fear.

Therefore, no marvel though Demetrius

Do as a monster fly my presence thus.

What wicked and dissembling glass of mine

Made me compare with Hermia's sphery eyne?

But who is here? Lysander! On the ground!

Dead? Or asleep? I see no blood, no wound.

Lysander, if you live, good sir, awake.

(Lysander declares his love for Helena).

Do not say so, Lysander, say not so.

What though he love your Hermia? Lord, what though?

Yet Hermia still loves you: then be content.

(Helena believes Lysander is mocking her. She doesn't realise he is under the influence of the love potion).

Wherefore was I to this keen mockery born?

When at your hands did I deserve this scorn?

Is't not enough, is't not enough, young man,

That I did never, no, nor never can,

Deserve a sweet look from Demetrius' eye,

But you must flout my insufficiency?

Good troth, you do me wrong – good sooth, you do –

In such disdainful manner me to woo.

But fair you well. Perforce I must confess

I thought you lord of more true gentleness.

O that a lady of one man refused,

Should of another therefore be abused.

A MIDSUMMER NIGHT'S DREAM ACT 3, SC 2

(Helena believes that Hermia, Lysander and Demetrius have been plotting against her)

<u>Helena:</u>

Lo, she is one of this confederacy!

Now I perceive they have conjoin'd all three

To fashion this false sport, in spite of me.

Injurious Hermia, most ungrateful maid!

Have you conspired, have you with these contrived

To bait me with this foul derision?

Is all the counsel that we two have shared,

The sisters' vows, the hours that we have spent,

When we have chid the hasty-footed time

For parting us, - O, is all forgot?

All school days' friendship, all childhood innocence?

We, Hermia, like two artificial gods,

Have with our needles created both one flower,

Both on one sampler, sitting on one cushion,

Both warbling of one song, both in one key,

As if our hands, our sides, voices and minds,

Had been incorporate. So, we grew together,

Like to a double cherry, seeming parted,

But yet an union in partition;

Two lovely berries moulded on one stem;

So, with two seeming bodies, but one heart;

Two of the first, like coats in heraldry,

Due but to one and crowned with one crest.

And will you rent our ancient love asunder,

To join with men in scorning your poor friend?

It is not friendly, 'tis not maidenly:

Our sex, as well as I, may chide you for it,

Though I alone do feel the injury

A MIDSUMMER NIGHT'S DREAM ACT 3, SC 2

(Hermia is demanding Demetrius tell her where Lysander is).

<u>Hermia:</u>

Now I but chide, but I should use thee worse,

For thou, I fear, hast given cause to curse.

If thou hast slain Lysander in his sleep,

Being o'er in blood plunge in the deep,

And kill me too.

The sun was not so true unto the day

As he to me. Would he have stolen away

From sleeping Hermia? I'll believe as soon

As this whole earth may be bored, and the moon

May through the centre creep, and so displease

Her brothers' noontide, with the Antipodes;

It cannot be but thou hast murdered him;

So should a murderer look so dead, so grim.

Oh, good Demetrius, wilt thou give him to me?

Out dog! Out cur! Thou driv'st me past the bounds

Of maiden's patience. Hast thou slain him?

Henceforth never be numbered among men!

O tell true- tell true, e'en for my sake;

Durst thou have looked upon him being awake,

And hast thou killed him sleeping? O brave touch

Could not a worm, an adder, do so much?

An adder did it; for with a doubler tongue

Than thine, thou serpent, never adder stung.

I pray thee, tell me then that he is well.

And from thy hated presence part I so;

See me no more, whether he be dead or no.

A MIDSUMMER NIGHT'S DREAM ACT 3, SC 2

(Hermia is defending herself against Helena's accusations)

<u>Hermia:</u>

I am amazed at your passionate words;

I scorn you not; it seems that you scorn me.

(Helena accuses Hermia of betraying her).

I understand not what you mean by this.

(Hermia discovers that Lysander is in love with Helena).

Oh me! You juggler, you canker-blossom,

You thief of love! What, have you come by night

And stolen my love's heart from him?

(Helena insults Hermia further, referring to her small stature).

Puppet? Why so! Ay, that way goes the game.

Now I perceive that she hath made compare

Between our statures; she hath urged her height,

And with her personage, her tall personage,

Her height, forsooth, she hath prevailed with him.

And are you grown so high in his esteem

Because I am so dwarfish and so low?

How low am I, thou painted maypole? Speak,

How low am I? I am not yet so low

But that my nails can reach unto thine eyes.

(Helena throws further insults at Hermia).

Little again? Nothing but low and little?

Why will you suffer her to flout me thus?

Let me come to her.

A MIDSUMMER NIGHT'S DREAM ACT 2, SC 1

(A Fairy meets Puck in a wood near Athens. The fairy is part of Titania, the Queen of the Fairies, entourage).

<u>Fairy:</u>

Over hill, over dale,
Thorough bush, thorough brier,
Over park, over pale,
Thorough flood, thorough fire,
I do wander everywhere,
Swifter than the moon's sphere;
And I serve the fairy queen,
To dew her orbs upon the green.
The cowslips tall her pensioners be:
In their gold coats spots you see;
Those be rubies, fairy favours,
In those freckles live their savours:
I must go seek some dewdrops here
And hang a pearl in every cowslip's ear.
Farewell, thou lob of spirits; I'll be gone:
Our queen and all our elves come here anon.
Either I mistake your shape and making quite,
Or else you are that shrewd and knavish sprite
Call'd Robin Goodfellow: are not you he
That frights the maidens of the villagery;
Skim milk, and sometimes labour in the quern
And bootless make the breathless housewife churn;
And sometime make the drink to bear no barm;
Mislead night-wanderers, laughing at their harm?
Those that Hobgoblin call you and sweet Puck,
You do their work, and they shall have good luck:
Are not you he?

Shakespeare Scenes

A MIDSUMMER NIGHT'S DREAM ACT 2, SC 1

(Puck meets a Fairy in a wood near Athens. Puck is Oberon's servant. Oberon is the King of the Spirit world).

Puck:

The king doth keep his revels here to-night:
Take heed the queen come not within his sight;
For Oberon is passing fell and wrath,
Because that she as her attendant hath
A lovely boy, stolen from an Indian king;
She never had so sweet a changeling;
And jealous Oberon would have the child
Knight of his train, to trace the forests wild;
But she perforce withholds the loved boy,
Crowns him with flowers and makes him all her joy:
And now they never meet in grove or green,
By fountain clear, or spangled starlight sheen,
But, they do square, that all their elves for fear
Creep into acorn-cups and hide them there.

Thou speak'st aright;
I am that merry wanderer of the night.
I jest to Oberon and make him smile
When I a fat and bean-fed horse beguile,
Neighing in likeness of a filly foal:
And sometime lurk I in a gossip's bowl,
In very likeness of a roasted crab,
And when she drinks, against her lips I bob
And on her wither'd dewlap pour the ale,
The wisest aunt, telling the saddest tale,
Sometime for three-foot stool mistaketh me;
Then slip I from her bum, down topples she,
And 'tailor' cries, and falls into a cough;

And then the whole quire hold their hips and laugh,
And waxen in their mirth and neeze and swear

A merrier hour was never wasted there.
But, room, fairy! here comes Oberon.

A MIDSUMMER NIGHT'S DREAM ACT 2, SC 2

(Puck has been ordered by Oberon to squeeze a love potion into the Athenian's eyes. Little does he know, he has chosen the wrong Athenian)

<u>Puck:</u>

Through the forest have I gone,

But Athenian found I none

On whose eyes I might approve

This flower's force in stirring love.

Night and silence: who is here?

Weeds of Athens he doth wear:

This is he, my master said,

Despised the Athenian maid:

And here the maiden, sleeping sound,

On the dank and dirty ground.

Pretty soul, she durst not lie

Near this lack-love, this kill-courtesy.

Churl, upon thy eyes I throw

All the power this charm doth owe:

When thou wak'st let love forbid

Sleep his seat on thy eyelid.

So awake when I am gone;

For I must now to Oberon.

A MIDSUMMER NIGHT'S DREAM ACT 3, Sc 2

(Oberon has ordered Puck to squeeze a remedial love juice into Lysanders' eyes. The spirit world will put their mischief to rights. Lysander will now fall back in love with Hermia).

<u>Puck:</u>

On the ground

Sleep sound;

I'll apply

To your eye,

Gentle lover, remedy. *(Puck squeezes the juice on Lysander's eyes)*

When thou wak'st,

Thou tak'st

True delight

In the sight

Of thy former lady's eye;

And the country proverb known,

That every man should take his own,

In your waking shall be shown:

Jack shall have Jill;

Nought shall go ill;

The man shall have his mare again,

And all shall be well.

A MIDSUMMER NIGHT'S DREAM ACT 5 SC 1

(Puck makes the final speech in the play and asks forgiveness from the audience)

Puck:

If we shadows have offended,

Think but this, and all is mended,

That you have but slumbered here,

While these visions did appear.

And this weak and idle theme,

No more yielding but a dream,

Gentles, do not reprehend:

If you pardon, we will mend.

And, as I am an honest Puck,

If we have unearned luck

Now to escape the serpent's tongue,

We will make amends 'ere long,

Else the Puck a liar call.

So, good night unto you all.

Give me your hands, if we be friends,

And Robin shall restore amends.

A MIDSUMMER NIGHT'S DREAM. ACT 3, SC 2

(Puck has followed Oberon's orders and applied the love potion to Titania's eyes)

Puck:

My mistress with a monster is in love.

Near to her close and consecrated bower

While she was in her dull and sleeping hour

A crew of patches, rude mechanicals

That work for bread upon Athenian stalls,

Were met together to rehearse a play

Intended for great Theseus' nuptial day.

The shallowest thickskin of that barren sort,

Who Pyramus presented, in their sport

Forsook his scene and entered in a brake,

When I did him at this advantage take.

An ass's nole I fixed on his head.

Anon his Thisbe must be answered,

And forth my mimic comes. When they him spy –

As wild geese that the creeping fowler eye,

Or russet-pated choughs, many in sort,

Rising and cawing at the gun's report,

Sever themselves and madly sweep the sky –

So, at his sight, away his fellows fly;

And at our stamp here o'er and o'er one falls.

He "Murder" cries, and help from Athens calls.

Their sense thus weak, lost with their fears thus strong,

Made senseless things begin to do them wrong.

For briers and thorns at their apparel snatch;

Some sleeves, some hats – from yielders all things catch.

I led them on in this distracted fear,

And left sweet Pyramus translated there;

When in that moment, so it came to pass,

Titania waked and straightway loved an ass.

A MIDSUMMER NIGHT'S DREAM ACT 3, SC 1

(Titania, Queen of the Fairies, has been put under a spell to make her fall in love with the first thing she lays eyes on upon. This happens to be Nick Bottom, who is sporting a pair of donkey ears).

Titania:

What angel wakes me from my flowery bed?

I pray thee, gentle mortal, sing again!

Mine ear is much enamour'd of thy note;

So is mine eye enthralled to thy shape;

And thy fair virtue's force, perforce, doth move me,

On the first view, to say, to swear, I love thee.

Thou art as wise as thou art beautiful.

Out of this wood do not desire to go:

Thou shalt remain here, whether thou wilt or no.

I am a spirit of no common rate;

The summer still doth tend upon my state;

And I do love thee: therefore, go with me:

I'll give you fairies to attend on thee,

And they shall fetch thee jewels from the deep,

And sing, while thou on pressed flowers dost sleep:

And I will purge thy mortal grossness so

That thou shalt like an airy spirit go.

(She speaks to four fairies)

Pease-blossom! Cobweb! Moth! And Mustard-seed!

Be kind and courteous to this gentle-man;

Hop in his walks, and gambol in his eyes;

Feed him with apricocks and dewberries,

With purple grapes, green figs, and mulberries.

The honey-bags steal from the honey-bees,

And for night-tapers crop their waxen thighs,

And light them at the fiery glow-worm's eyes:

Nod to him, elves, do him courtesies.

Come, wait upon him; lead him to my bower.

The moon methinks, looks with a watery eye;

And when she weeps, weeps every little flower,

Lamenting some enforced chastity.

Tie up my love's tongue, bring him silently.

Shakespeare Scenes

AS YOU LIKE IT

As You Like It is a romantic comedy most of which is set in the Forest of Arden. There are two Dukes. The older, more popular Duke, has been banished by the younger, Duke Frederick. He has a daughter called Rosalind. Duke Frederick's daughter is called Celia. The two girls are inseparable. The Duke decides to banish Rosalind due to her popularity and on hearing this, Celia decides to accompany her. Rosalind disguises herself as a boy, for safety and they take the fool, Touchstone with them. Prior to this banishment, Rosalind has fallen in love with Orlando who has also had to run away to the forest to escape his jealous, older brother, Oliver. Whilst in the forest, Rosalind discovers that Orlando is there too but cannot pursue a relationship with him as she is now in disguise. Much comedy ensues due to mistaken identity. Later, when Rosalind discovers that Orlando has been injured trying to save his brother, Oliver, from a lion, Rosalind faints and reveals herself. Oliver redeems himself and falls in love with Celia. Touchstone marries Audrey and the shepherds, Phoebe and Silvius also marry. Duke Frederick, on seeking out his brother in order to murder him, is converted by a hermit and decides to leave his Dukedom to the old Duke. A large wedding takes place and everyone lives happily ever after.

Shakespeare Scenes

AS YOU LIKE IT ACT 3, SC 5

(Phoebe, a shepherdess, is speaking to Silvius, a shepherd in love with her. However, Phoebe has just met Rosalind disguised as Gannymede and is infatuated with him!)

Phoebe:

Know'st thou the youth that spoke to me ere while?

Think not I love him, though I ask for him;

'Tis but a peevish boy: yet he talks well;-

But what care I for words? yet words do well,

When he that speaks them pleases those that hear.

'Tis a pretty youth: - not very pretty: -

But, sure, he's proud; and yet his pride becomes him:

He'll make a proper man! The best thing in him

Is his complexion; and faster than his tongue

Did make offence, his eye did heal it up.

He is not tall; yet for his years he's tall:

His leg is but so so; and yet 't is well:

There was a pretty redness in his lip;

A little riper and more lusty red

Than that mixed in his cheek; 't was just the difference

Betwixt the constant red and mingled damask.

There be some women, Silvius, had they marked him

In parcels as I did, would have gone near

To fall in love with him: but, for my part,

I love him not, nor hate him not; and yet

I have more cause to hate him than to love him;

For what had he to do to chide at me?

He said, mine eyes were black, and mine hair black;

And now, I am remembered, scorned at me:

I marvel why I answered not again:

But that's all one; omittance is no quittance.

I'll write to him a very taunting letter,

And thou shalt bear it: wilt thou, Silvius?

I'll write it straight;

The matter's in my head, and in my heart:

I will be bitter with him, and passing short.

Go with me, Silvius.

AS YOU LIKE IT ACT 3, SC 2

(Phoebe, a shepherdess, is speaking to Silvius. Silvius, the shepherd is in love with Phoebe. However, Phoebe has just met Rosalind disguised as Gannymede and has become infatuated with her/him!)

Phoebe:

I would not be thy executioner;

I fly thee, for I would not injure thee.

Thou tell'st me, there is murder in mine eye:

'T is pretty, sure, and very probable,

That eyes, - that are the frail'st and softest things,

Who shut their coward gates on atomies, -

Should be called tyrants, butchers, murderers!

Now I do frown on thee; with all my heart;

And if mine eyes can wound, now let them kill thee;

Now counterfeit to swoon; why now fall down;

Or it thou can'st not, O, for shame, for shame,

Lie not, to say mine eyes are murderers.

Now shew the wound mine eye hath made in thee:

Scratch thee but with a pin, and there remains

Some scar of it: lean but upon a rush,

The cicatrice and capable impressure

Thy palm some moment keeps: but now mine eyes

Which I have darted at thee, hurt thee not;

Nor, I am sure, there is no force in eyes

That can do hurt.

    But till that time

Come not thou near me: and when that time comes

Afflict me with thy mocks, pity me not;

As, till that time, I shall not pity thee.

AS YOU LIKE IT ACT 3, SC 3

(The scene takes place in the forest. Rosalind is in love with Orlando. As she is disguised as a boy named Ganymede, he does not recognize her. In this scene, Rosalind teases Orlando. She tells him he can't possibly know what it is to be in love).

Rosalind:

There is none of my uncle's marks upon you. He taught me how to know a man in love; in which cage of rushes I am sure you are not a prisoner. A lean cheek, which you have not; a blue eye and sunken, which you have not; an unquestionable spirit, which, you have not; a beard neglected, which you have not – but I pardon you for that, for simply your having in beard is a younger brother's revenue. Then your hose should be ungartered, your bonnet unbanded, your sleeve unbuttoned, your shoe untied, and everything about you demonstrating a careless desolation. But you are no such man: you are rather point-device in your accoutrements, as loving yourself than seeming the lover of any other. But in good sooth, are you he that hangs the verses on the trees, wherein Rosalind is so admired?

AS YOU LIKE IT ACT 3, SC 5

(Rosalind overhears the shepherdess, Phoebe, insulting the shepherd, Silvius and decides to put Phoebe in her place. Phoebe immediately develops a crush on Rosalind, believing her to be a man).

Rosalind:

And why, I pray you?

Who might be your mother,

That you insult, exult, and all at once,

Over the wretched?

What though you have no beauty –

As, by my faith, I see no more in you

Than without candle may go dark to bed –

Must you be therefore proud and pitiless?

Why, what means this? Why do you look on me?

I see no more in you than in the ordinary

Of nature's sale-work. ('Ods my little life,

I think she means to tangle my eyes too!)

No, faith, proud mistress, hope not after it:

'Tis not your inky brows, your black silk hair,

Your bugle eyeballs, nor your cheek of cream,

That can entame my spirits to your worship.

You, foolish shepherd, wherefore do you follow her,

Like foggy south puffing with wind and rain?

You are a thousand times a properer man

Than she a woman: 'tis such fools as you

That makes the world full of ill-favored children:

'Tis not her glass, but you, that flatters her;

And out of you she sees herself more proper

Than any of her lineaments can show her.

But mistress, know yourself: down on your knees

And thank heaven, fasting, for a good man's love:

For I must tell you friendly in your ear,

Sell when you can: you are not for all markets:

Cry the man mercy; love him; take his offer:

Foul is most foul, being foul to be a scoffer.

So, take her to thee, shepherd: fare you well.

(to herself).

He's fallen in love with her foulness, and she'll fall in love with my anger. If it be so, as fast as she answers thee with frowning looks, I'll sauce her with bitter words. – *(To Phoebe)* Why look you so upon me?

I pray you, do not fall in love with me,

For I am falser than vows made in wine;

Besides, I like you not. If you will know my house,

'Tis at the tuft of olives, here hard by. –

(To Sylvius). Shepherd, ply her hard –

Shepherdess, look on him better,

And be not proud; though all the world could see,

None could be so abused in sight as he.

THE TEMPEST

The Tempest is a magical comedy, although at times, it can seem quite dark due to the tumultuous Tempest which Ariel has created for his master, Prospero. Prospero's daughter, 15yr old Miranda, watches the storm in horror, afraid that those affected by the shipwreck will lose their lives. Prospero has his own good reasons for bringing the ship and its guests to the island and therefore ensures that no one is harmed. Prospero, a great magician, was formerly the Duke of Milan. His evil brother, Antonio attempted to overthrow him but fortunately, Prospero and his baby daughter escaped. For twelve years they have lived on the island but now Prospero deems it is time to resolve matters. Prospero conjures a spell for Miranda to fall in love with Prince Ferdinand. The King of Naples, Antonio and his sailors have all been scattered about the island, each believing the other to be dead. The spirit, Ariel, casts spells on the visitors, inducing sleep, to affect the endgame. There is also an evil fish-like creature called Caliban whom Prospero keeps locked up as a slave. Desiring revenge on Prospero, Caliban attempts to manipulate Trinculo and Stephano to help him kill Prospero so that the three of them can rule the island. Prospero's magic spell ensures that Ferdinand and Miranda meet, fall instantly in love and decide to get married. Prospero yearns for the life that was intended for Miranda. He also feels the need to go back to the real world and leave his magic behind him. Finally, Antonio is repentant and Prospero is restored as the Duke of Milan and his lands are returned. The king of Naples welcomes Miranda as his daughter in law. Ariel, his faithful spirit has earned his promised freedom. As in all comedies, there is a very happy ending.

Shakespeare Scenes

THE TEMPEST ACT 1, SC 2

(Ariel is telling his master, Prospero, that he has created a magnificent Tempest. He hopes this will earn him his freedom).

Ariel:

I boarded the King's Ship. Now on the beak,

Now in the waist, the deck, in every cabin,

I flamed amazement. Sometimes I'd divide,

And burn in many places. On the topmast,

The yards and bowsprit would I flame distinctly,

Then meet and join. Jove's lightnings, the precursors

O' the dreadful thunderclaps, more momentary

And sight-outrunning were not. The fire and cracks

Of sulphurous roaring the most mighty Neptune

Seemed to besiege, and make his bold waves

Tremble – Yea, his dread trident shake.

Not a soul but felt a fever of the mad, and played

Some tricks of desperation. All but mariners

Plunged in the foaming brine, and quit the vessel,

Then all afire with me. The King's son, Ferdinand,

With hair up-staring – then like reeds, not hair –

Was the first man that leaped: cried, 'Hell is empty,

And all the devils are here!'

Not a hair perished:

On their sustaining garments not a blemish,

But fresher than before. And, as thou bad'st me,

In troops, I have dispersed them 'bout the isle.

The King's son have I landed by himself –

Whom I left cooling of the air with sighs

In an odd angle of the isle, and sitting,

His arms in this sad knot.

THE TEMPEST ACT 1, SC 2

(Miranda questions her father, Prospero about the recent storm and about her past life before they came to the island)

Miranda:

If by your art, my dearest father, you have

Put the wild waters in this roar, allay them.

The sky, it seems would pour down stinking pitch

But that the sea, mounting to th'welkin's cheek,

Dashes the fire out. O, I have suffer'd

With those that I saw suffer: a brave vessel –

Who had, no doubt, some noble creature in her –

Dash'd all to pieces! O, the cry did knock

Against my very heart – poor souls, they perish'd.

Had I been any god of power, I would

Have sunk the sea within the earth 'ere

It should the good ship so have swallow'd, and

The fraughting souls within her.

(She sits)

                                               You have often

Begun to tell me what I am, but stopp'd,

And left me to a bootless inquisition,

Concluding, 'Stay, not yet.'

'Tis far off,

And rather like a dream than an assurance

That my remembrance warrants. Had I not

Four or five women once that tended me?

Sir, are you not my father?

                                        O, the heavens!

What foul play had we that we came from thence?

Or blessed was't we did?

                                        O, my heart bleeds

To think o'th'teen that I have turn'd you to,

Which is from my remembrance. Please you, farther.

                                        Your tale, sir, would cure deafness.

TEMPEST ACT 3, SC 1

(Miranda meets Ferdinand for the first time. Prospero has put a spell on both of them to ensure they fall in love with each other)

<u>Miranda:</u>

Alas, now, pray you,

Work not so hard: I would, the lightning had,

Burn't up those logs that you are enjoin'd to pile.

Pray, set it down, and rest you: when this burns,

'T will weep for having wearied you. My father

Is hard at study: pray now, rest yourself:

He's safe for these three hours.

(Miranda offers to help Ferdinand).

If you'll sit down,

I'll bear your logs the while. Pray, give me that:

I'll carry it to the pile. It would become me

As well as it does you: and I should do it

With much more ease, for my good will is to it,

And yours it is against.

(After carrying the logs, Miranda introduces herself).

My name is Miranda ;- *(To herself)* O my father!

I have broke your hest, to say so.

I do not know

One of my sex; no woman's face remember,

Save, from my glass, mine own; nor have I seen

More than I may call men, than thou, good friend,

And my dear father; how features are abroad,

I am skill-less of:

> (*To herself*) But I prattle

Something too wildly, and my father's precepts

I therein do forget.

(To Ferdinand).

Do you love me?

(Ferdinand replies that he does love Miranda).

I am a fool,

To weep at what I am glad of.

> (*To herself*) But this is trifling;

And all the more it seeks to hide itself,

The bigger bulk it shows. Hence, bashful cunning!

And prompt me, plain and holy innocence!

(To Ferdinand)

I am your wife, if you will marry me;

If not, I'll die your maid; to be your fellow

You may deny me; but I'll be your servant,

Whether you will or no.

(Ferdinand agrees to marry her).

My husband then? and now farewell,

Till half an hour hence.

TEMPEST ACT 3, SC 3

(Ariel enters accompanied by thunder and lightning. He addresses Alonso, Sebastian and Gonzalo).

<u>Ariel:</u>

You are three men of sin, whom Destiny,

That hath to instrument this lower world

And what is in't, the never-surfeited sea

Hath caus'd to belch up you, and on this island,

Where man doth not inhabit – you 'mongst men

Being most unfit to live. I have made you mad;

And even with such-like valour men hang and drown

Their proper selves.

(The men draw their swords)

You fools! And my fellows

Are ministers of Fate – the elements

Of whom your swords are temper'd may as well

Wound the loud winds, or with bemock'd-at stabs

Kill the still-closing waters, as diminish

One dowl that's in my plume. My fellow ministers

Are like invulnerable. If you could hurt,

Your swords are now too massy for your strengths,

And will not be uplifted. But remember –

For that's my business to you – that you three

From Milan did supplant good Prospero,

Expos'd unto the sea, which hath requit it,

Him and his innocent child; for which foul deed,

The powers delaying, not forgetting, have

Incens'd the seas and shores, yea all the creatures

Against your peace. Thee of thy son, Alonso,

They have bereft; and do pronounce by me

Ling'ring perdition, worse that any death

Can be at once, shall step by step attend

You and your ways; whose wraths to guard you from,

Which here, in this most desolate isle, else falls

Upon your heads, is nothing but heart's sorrow,

And a clear life ensuing.

(Ariel vanishes)

Shakespeare Scenes

TWELFTH NIGHT

Twelfth Night is a romantic comedy which takes place on an island called Illyria. Identical twins, Viola and Sebastian, have been in a terrible storm and have been separated during a shipwreck. They have been washed ashore on the island, supposing each other has drowned.

In order to protect herself in a strange land, Viola disguises herself as a young man and finds employment in the Count Orsino's household, where she promptly falls in love with her employer. Orsino is in love with the Countess Olivia and sends his servant, Viola to woo her. Olivia does not love Orsino but does, however, fall in love with Viola (male name Cesario).

There are some very amusing characters at Olivia's court; namely Malvolio, Sir Toby Belch and Sir Andrew Aguecheek. These characters provide much of the comedy and form the subplot of the play.

Meanwhile, Sebastian is still very much alive. When Olivia encounters him, she assumes him to be her love interest, Viola. Further comedy arises when Viola meets the sea captain, Antonio, who supposes she is her identical twin, Sebastian. Eventually, all is resolved. Viola is reunited with her lost brother. Olivia is more than happy to marry Sebastian, which frees up Viola to reveal her true identity and thus, pursue her love for Orsino.

Shakespeare Scenes

Shakespeare Scenes

TWELFTH NIGHT ACT 1, SC 5

(Viola, dressed as a manservant to the Duke Orsino, has been commissioned to pay homage to the Countess Olivia. Olivia refuses Orsino's declaration of love but comically falls in love with Viola)

Viola:

The honourable lady of the house, which is she?

Most radiant, exquisite, and unmatchable beauty - I pray you tell me if this be the lady of the house, for I never saw her. I would be loath to cast away my speech: for besides that it is excellently well penned, I have taken great pains to con it. Good beauties, let me sustain no scorn; I am very comptible, even to the least sinister usage.

Good gentle one, give me modest assurance if you be the lady of the house, that I may proceed in my speech.

Are you the lady of the house?

Most certain, if you are she, you do usurp yourself; for what is yours to bestow is not yours to reserve. But this is from my commission. I will on with my speech in your praise, and then show you the heart of my message.

It alone concerns your ear. I bring no overture of war, no taxation of homage; I hold the olive in my hand: my words are as full of peace, as matter.

The rudeness that hath appeared in me have I learned from my entertainment. What I am, and what I would, are as secret as maidenhead: to your ears, divinity; to any other's profanation.

Good madam, let me see your face.

Excellently done, if God did all.

'Tis beauty truly blent, whose red and white

Nature's own sweet and cunning hand laid on.

Lady, you are the cruell'st she alive

If you will lead these graces to the grave

And leave the world no copy.

TWELFTH NIGHT ACT 1, SC 5

(Viola, dressed as a manservant to the Duke Orsino, has been commissioned to pay homage to the Countess Olivia. Olivia refuses Orsino's declaration of love but falls in love with Viola)

<u>Viola:</u>

I see you what you are, you are too proud:

But if you were the devil, you are fair.

My lord and master loves you: O, such love

Could be but recompens'd, though you were crown'd

The nonpareil of beauty!

If I did love you in my master's flame,

With such a suff'ring, such a deadly life,

In your denial I would find no sense,

I would not understand it.

(Olivia asks Viola what she would do if she were in love).

Why what would I?

(Viola replies, all the while thinking of her love for Duke Orsino).

Make me a willow cabin at your gate,

And call upon my soul within the house;

Write loyal cantons of contemned love,

And sing them loud even in the dead of night;

Halloo your name to the reverberate hills,

And make the babbling gossip of the air

Cry out 'Olivia!' O, you should not rest

Between the elements of air and earth,

But you should pity me.

(Olivia tries to give Viola some money for her services).

I am no fee'd post, lady; keep your purse.

My master, not myself, lacks recompense.

Love make his heart of flint that you shall love,

And let your fervour like my master's be

Plac'd in contempt. Farewell, fair cruelty.

TWELFTH NIGHT ACT 2, SC 2

(Olivia, presuming Viola is a male messenger, named Cesario, has fallen in love with her. Olivia has sent her servant, Malvolio, with a ring as a token of her love for Cesario)

<u>Viola:</u>

I left no ring with her. What means this lady?

Fortune forbid my outside have not charmed her.

She made good view of me, indeed so much

That sure methought her eyes had lost her tongue,

For she did speak in starts, distractedly.

She loves me, sure. The cunning of her passion

Invites me in this churlish messenger.

None of my lord's ring! Why, he sent her none.

I am the man. If it be so – as 'tis –

Poor lady, she were better love a dream!

Disguise, I see thou art a wickedness

Wherein the pregnant enemy does much.

How easy is it for the proper false

In women's waxen hearts to set their forms!

Alas, our frailty is the cause, not we,

For such as we are made of, such we be.

How will this fadge? My master loves her dearly,

And I, poor monster, fond as much on him;

And she, mistaken, seems to dote on me.

What will become of this? As I am man,

My state is desperate for my master's love.

As I am woman, now, alas the day!

What thriftless sighs shall poor Olivia breathe!

O time, thou must untangle this, not I.

It is too hard a knot for me t'untie.

TWELFTH NIGHT ACT 1, SC 5

(Viola is acting as a messenger for the Duke Orsino. Her job is to declare Orsino's love to Olivia. Olivia is not amused and gives Viola, short shrift)

Olivia:

Give me my veil: come, throw it o'er my face.

We'll once more hear Orsino's embassy.

(Olivia is now wearing a black veil, in mourning).

Speak to me, I shall answer for her. Your will?

I heard you were saucy at my gates, and allowed

your approach rather to wonder at you than to hear

you. If you be not mad, be gone: If you have reason, be

brief. 'Tis not that time of moon with me to make

one in so skipping a dialogue.

Speak your office.

What are you? What would you?

Give us this place alone: we will hear this divinity.

(Olivia's attendants leave)

Now, sir, what is your text?

Oh, I have read it: it is heresy. Have you no more to say?

Have you any commission from your lord to negotiate with my face? You are now out of your text: but we will draw the curtain and show you the picture. Look you, sir, such a one I was this present. Is't not well done?

I will give out divers schedules of my beauty. It shall be inventoried, and every particle and utensil labelled to my will. As item: two lips indifferent red; item: two grey eyes, with lids to them; item: One neck, one chin, and so forth. Were you sent hither to praise me?

TWELFTH NIGHT ACT 1, SC 5

(Viola is acting as a messenger for the Duke Orsino. She declares Orsino's love to Olivia. Olivia is not amused and gives Viola, short shrift. She tells Viola that she is not in love with Orsino).

Olivia:

Your lord does know my mind, I cannot love him.

Yet I suppose him virtuous, know him noble,

Of great estate, of fresh and stainless youth;

In voices well divulg'd, free, learn'd and valiant,

and in dimension, and in the shape of nature,

A gracious person: but yet I cannot love him.

He might have took his answer long ago.

           Get you to your lord:

I cannot love him: let him send no more –

Unless, perchance, you come to me again,

To tell me how he takes it. Fare you well.

I thank you for your pains, spend this for me.

(Viola exits. Olivia reveals that she has fallen in love with Viola).

'What is your parentage?"

'Above my fortune yet my state is well;

I am a gentleman'. I'll be sworn thou art:

Thy tongue, thy face, thy limbs, actions, and spirit

Do give thee five-fold blazon. Not too fast: Soft! soft!

Unless the master were the man! How now?

Even so quickly may one catch the plague?

Methinks I feel this youth's perfections

With an invisible and subtle stealth

To creep in at mine eyes. Well, let it be.

TWELFTH NIGHT ACT 3, SC 1

(Olivia has fallen in love with Viola, believing him to be a young man, named Cesario).

<u>Olivia:</u>

O world! How apt the poor are to be proud.

If one should be a prey, how much the better

To fall before the lion than the wolf!

The clock upbraids me with the waste of time.

Be not afraid, good youth. I will not have you;

And yet, when wit and youth is come to harvest,

Your wife is like to reap a proper man:

There lies your way, due west.

                              But stay:

I prithee, tell me what thou think'st of me.

O! what a deal of scorn looks beautiful

In the contempt and anger of his lip.

A murderous guilt shows not itself more soon

Than love that would seem hid love's night is noon.

Cesario, by the roses of the spring,

By maidhood, honour, truth, and everything,

I love thee so, that, maugre all thy pride,

Nor wit nor reason can my passion hide.

Do not extort thy reasons from this clause,

For that I woo, thou therefore hast no cause;

But rather reason thus with reason fetter,

Love sought is good, but giv'n unsought is better.

THE TWO GENTLEMEN OF VERONA

The Two Gentlemen of Verona is a romantic comedy. The two gentlemen of the story are Valentine and Proteus. Valentine is leaving for Milan to study. Proteus meanwhile, is pursuing a relationship with a young woman named Julia. He sends her a letter, via Valentine's servant, Speed. Speed passes this letter on to Julia's lady in waiting, Lucetta. Julia sends a letter in reply but when Proteus's father, Antonio, sees his son reading it, Proteus tells his father that it is from his friend, Valentine. His father, Antonio decides that it is time for his son to resume his studies in Milan too. In Milan, Valentine spends much of his time wooing a beautiful lady named Silvia rather than studying. When Proteus visits Milan, he soon forgets his loyalty to Julia, as well as to his friend, Valentine, and falls in love with Sylvia. Now Sylvia has three suitors: Valentine, Thurio and Proteus. Julia, pining for Proteus, decides to travel to Milan, disguised as a page. When Proteus discovers that Valentine and Sylvia plan to elope together, he tells Sylvia's father and Valentine is banished. Julia soon finds out that Proteus is paying attentions to Sylvia. She becomes Proteus' page and in her duties is sent with a ring to Sylvia. Julia tells Sylvia that Proteus already has a lover back in Verona and Sylvia is most sympathetic in her response. Sylvia does not love Proteus and is planning to run away to the forest in order to find Valentine. On discovering this, Proteus decides to follow her, closely followed by Julia. Proteus finds Sylvia and declares his love to her but Valentine intervenes and stops him. Julia consequently faints and her true identity is revealed. Proteus immediately sees the error of his way and declares his love for Julia, leaving Valentine free to marry Sylvia. The Duke of Milan happens to be passing by and graciously forgives everyone, creating a happy ending.

Shakespeare Scenes

THE TWO GENTLEMEN OF VERONA ACT 1, SC 2

(Julia is talking to her waiting woman, Lucetta. She discovers that Lucetta has a love letter for her, from Proteus)

Julia:

But say, Lucetta, now we are alone,

Wouldst thou then counsel me to fall in love?

Of all the fair resort of gentlemen

That every day with parle encounter me,

In thy opinion which is worthiest love?

What thinkest thou of the fair Sir Eglamour?

What thinkest thou of the rich Mercatio?

What thinkest thou of the gentle Proteus?

And wouldst thou have me cast my love on him?

Why, he, of all the rest, hath never moved me.

(Julia realizes that Lucetta has a letter).

What paper, madam?

To Julia, say, from whom?

Say, say, who gave it thee?

Now, by my modesty, a goodly broker!

Dare you presume to harbour wanton lines?

To whisper and conspire against my youth?

Now, trust me, 'tis an office of great worth,

And you an officer fit for the place.

There take the paper. See it be returned,

Or else return no more into my sight.

(*Lucetta leaves*).

(*Julia now considers the letter*)

And yet I would I had o'erlooked the letter.

It were a shame to call her back again,

And pray her to a fault for which I chid her.

What 'fool is she, that knows I am a maid,

And would not force the letter to my view,

Since maids, in modesty, say no to that

Which they would have the profferer construe ay.

Fie, fie! How wayward is this foolish love,

That, like a testy babe, will scratch the nurse,

And presently, all humbled, kiss the rod.

How churlishly I chid Lucetta hence,

When willingly I would have had her here.

How angerly I taught my brow to frown,

When inward joy enforced my heart to smile.

My penance is to call Lucetta back

THE TWO GENTLEMEN OF VERONA ACT 1, SC 2

(Lucetta drops the letter which Proteus has written to Julia)

Julia:

(To Lucetta)

Go get you gone, and let the papers lie.

You would be fingering them, to anger me.

(Alone)

O, hateful hands, to tear such loving words.

Injurious wasps, to feed on such sweet honey,

And kill the bees that yield it with your stings.

I'll kiss each several paper for amends.

Look, here is writ, *kind Julia.* Unkind Julia,

As in revenge of thy ingratitude,

I throw thy name against the bruising stones,

Trampling contemptuously on thy disdain.

And here is writ, *love-wounded Proteus.*

Poor wounded name, my bosom, as a bed,

Shall lodge thee till thy wound be thoroughly healed;

And thus I search it with a sovereign kiss.

But twice or thrice was Proteus written down.

Be calm, good wind, blow not a word away

Till I have found each letter in the letter,

Except mine own name. That some whirlwind bear

Unto a ragged, fearful, hanging rock,

And throw it thence into the raging sea.

Lo, here in one line is his name twice writ:

Poor, forlorn Proteus, passionate Proteus,

To the sweet Julia. That I'll tear away;

And yet I will not, since so prettily

He couples it to his complaining names.

Thus, will I fold them one upon another.

Now kiss, embrace, contend, do what you will.

THE TWO GENTLEMEN OF VERONA ACT 4 SC 4

(Sylvia has recently exited and Julia speaks alone. Julia knows that Proteus, has been flirting with Sylvia. She makes comparison between herself and Sylvia as she has Sylvia's picture).

<u>Julia:</u>

And she shall thank you for't, if e'er you know her. (*to Sylvia*)

A virtuous gentlewoman, mild and beautiful.

I hope my master's suit will be but cold,

Since she respects my mistress' love so much.

Alas, how love can trifle with itself!

Here is her picture. Let me see: I think,

If I had such a tire, this face of mine

Were full as lovely as is this of hers;

And yet the painter flatter'd her a little,

Unless I flatter with myself too much.

Her hair is auburn, mine is perfect yellow:

If that be all the difference in his love,

I'll get me such a colour'd periwig.

Her eyes are grey as glass, and so are mine:

Ay, but her forehead's low, and mine's as high,

What should it be, that he respects in her,

But I can make respective in myself,

If this fond Love were not a blinded god?

Come, shadow, come, and take this shadow up,

For 't is thy rival. O thou senseless form!

Thou shalt be worshipp'd, kiss'd, lov'd, and ador'd.

And, were there sense in his idolatry,

My substance should be statue in thy stead.

I'll use thee kindly for thy mistress' sake,

That us'd me so, or else, by Jove I vow,

I should have scratch'd out your unseeing eyes,

To make my master out of love with thee.

Shakespeare Scenes

THE MERCHANT OF VENICE

The Merchant of Venice is a romantic comedy. However, there are some very serious themes within the play regarding money, attempted murder, mercy and antisemitism. The play takes place in Venice, Italy. A merchant, named Antonio, wishes to lend his best friend, Bassanio, enough money (three thousand ducats) to woo the heiress, Portia. He borrows this money from the Jewish moneylender, Shylock. Shylock hates all Christians due to the ill treatment of Jews over the centuries. To make matters worse, his own daughter, Jessica, has fallen in love with a Christian, and later runs away with him. He agrees to lend the money to Antonio on condition that he signs an agreement that if the money is not paid after three months, Shylock can lawfully cut off a pound of Antonio's flesh.

Meanwhile, in Belmont, the beautiful heiress, Portia is receiving foreign suitors. The only suitor she is interested in is, the Venetian, Bassanio. A task has been set for these suitors to choose one of three caskets of gold, silver and lead. Portia's future husband will be the suitor who chooses the right casket which has her portrait inside it. Portia tries to delay Bassanio's choosing of the casket, concerned that he might fail to choose the right casket. Bassanio eventually chooses the lead casket, which includes the portrait of Portia.

Later in the play, Shylock learns that Antonio's ships have been wrecked and he is no longer able to repay the loan. This results in a lengthy Trial Scene where Shylock is determined to claim his revenge. However, Portia, desperate to save the situation, disguises herself as an out of town lawyer and saves the day on a technicality. She requests that Shylock act mercifully but Shylock refuses. He is determined to pursue his case according to Venetian law. Portia reminds Shylock that he will, in fact, be breaking Venetian law if he takes more than just a pound of flesh. He must not shed any blood in the transaction. If he does, by law, all his goods will be confiscated. Shylock has lost his case. All is resolved. Portia and Bassanio are wed. Her lady in waiting, Nerissa marries Gratiano and Jessica marries Lorenzo.

Shakespeare Scenes

MERCHANT OF VENICE ACT 2, SC 6

(Jessica, Shylock's daughter, dressed in boy's clothes is planning to run away from home with the Christian, Lorenzo).

Jessica:

Farewell, good Launcelot.

Alack, what heinous sin is in me

To be ashamed to be my father's child!

But though I am a daughter to his blood

I am not to his manners: O, Lorenzo,

If thou keep promise I shall end this strife,

Become a Christian and thy loving wife!

Farewell – and if my fortune be not crost,

I have a father, you a daughter, lost.

(Jessica shouts out to Lorenzo from the window)

Who are you? – tell me for more certainty,

Albeit I'll swear that I do know your tongue.

Lorenzo, certain, and my love indeed,

For who love I so much? And now who knows

But you, Lorenzo whether I am yours?

Here, catch this casket, it is worth the pains.

I am glad 'tis night – you do not look on me,

For I am much asham'd of my exchange:

But love is blind, and lovers cannot see

The pretty follies that themselves commit,

For if they could, Cupid himself would blush

To see me thus transformed to a boy.

(Lorenzo holds up a lamp to see Jessica).

What, must I hold a candle to my shames?

They in themselves, good sooth, are too, too light.

Why, 'tis an office of discovery, love,

And I should be obscured.

I will make fast the doors and gild myself

With some more ducats, and be with you straight.

(Jessica runs to collect some more coins & then returns to the window to escape with Lorenzo).

THE MERCHANT OF VENICE ACT 3, SC 2

(Bassanio has chosen the right casket and now Portia declares her love for Bassanio).

Portia:

You see me, Lord Bassanio, where I stand,

Such as I am. Though for myself alone

I would not be ambitious in my wish

To wish myself much better, yet for you

I would be trebled twenty times myself,

A thousand times more fair,

ten thousand times more rich,

That only to stand high in your account

I might in virtues, beauties, livings, friends,

Exceed account. But the full sum of me

Is sum of something which, to term in gross,

Is an unlessoned girl, unschooled, unpractised,

Happy in this, she is not yet so old

But she may learn; happier than this,

She is not bred so dull but she can learn;

Happiest of all is that her gentle spirit

Commits itself to yours to be directed

As from her lord, her governor, her king.

Myself and what is mine to you and yours

Is now converted. But now I was the lord

Of this fair mansion, master of my servants,

Queen o'er myself; and even now, but now,

This house, these servants, and this same myself

Are yours, my lords. I give them with this ring,

Which when you part from, lose, or give away,

Let it presage the ruin of your love,

And be my vantage to exclaim on you.

MERCHANT OF VENICE ACT 4, SC 1

(Portia speaks of the importance of mercy, during Shylock's trial scene)

Portia:

The quality of mercy is not strained,

It droppeth as the gentle rain from heaven

Upon the place beneath. It is twice blest:

It blesseth him that gives, and him that takes.

'Tis mightiest in the mightiest, it becomes

The throned monarch better than his crown.

His sceptre shows the force of temporal power,

The attribute to awe and majesty,

Wherein doth sit the dread and fear of kings;

But mercy is above this sceptre sway.

It is enthroned in the hearts of kings,

It is an attribute to God himself,

And earthly power doth then show likest God's

When mercy seasons justice. Therefore, Jew,

Though justice be thy plea, consider this:

That in the course of justice, none of us

Should see salvation. We do pray for mercy,

And that same prayer doth teach us all to render

The deeds of mercy. I have spoke thus much

To mitigate the justice of thy plea,

Which if thou follow, this strict court of Venice

Must needs give sentence 'gainst the merchant there.

HAMLET

Hamlet is a revenge tragedy. The play is set in Denmark at the Castle of Elsinore. The play begins with the ghost of the late King of Denmark walking the battlements, as if to warn his citizens of some imminent danger. There is a threat of war between neighboring Norway. Hamlet's friend, Horatio, sees the ghost and tells his best friend, Hamlet. Gertrude, the Queen, has married her husband's brother, Claudius, in less than two months of her husband's death. Hamlet is beside himself with grief and outrage. Polonius, the Lord Chamberlain, has a son, Laertes, and a beautiful daughter, Ophelia, whom Hamlet has been courting. Hamlet and Horatio visit the battlements with a view to seeing the ghost again. The ghost appears again and Hamlet learns that his father's death was most unnatural. He was poisoned by his own brother, Claudius. From this point on, Hamlet is distraught and determined for revenge. The court begin to worry about Hamlet's behaviour. Hamlet is rough in his treatment of Ophelia and kills her father, Polonius, for spying. Hamlet is also physically aggressive towards his mother, Gertrude. A group of travelling players visit the castle and Hamlet asks them to perform a play 'The Murder of Gonzago', which includes the poisoning of a King. Hamlet wants to see if his uncle reacts guiltily. Claudius fully obliges and it is clear to Hamlet that he is indeed guilty. Claudius's response to this is to remove Hamlet from Denmark. He asks Rosencrantz and Guildenstern to assist him in this task and to monitor Hamlet's movements. After Hamlet kills Polonius, he has a good excuse to send him to England. On the way there, Hamlet encounters the Prince of Norway. Meanwhile, the grief of losing her father and being spurned by Hamlet is too much for Ophelia and she loses her mind and shortly after takes her own life. On returning to England, Hamlet discovers on passing the graveyard that Ophelia is now dead. Laertes and Hamlet argue. Claudius directs Laertes to kill Hamlet by challenging him to a duel with a poisoned rapier.

There is also a poisoned chalice, but Hamlet, preoccupied with the duel does not drink it and the Queen takes sip from the chalice instead. The poisoned rapier changes hands and Laertes is poisoned. On realizing this, Hamlet seizes the sword and stabs the King. He then drinks the poisoned wine from the chalice himself. In Hamlet's dying speech, he hands his role over to Horatio, whilst also stating his wishes are for the Prince of Norway to rule Denmark.

HAMLET ACT 2, SC 1

(Ophelia is speaking to her father, Polonius. She tells him how she has been treated badly by Lord Hamlet).

<u>Ophelia:</u>

Alas, my lord, I have been so affrighted.

My lord, as I was sewing in my chamber,

Lord Hamlet, with his doublet all unbraced,

No hat upon his head, his stockings fouled,

Ungartered, and down-gyved to his ankle,

Pale as his shirt, his knees knocking each other,

And with a look so piteous in purport

As if he had been loosed out of hell

To speak of horrors, he comes before me.

He took me by the wrist and held me hard,

Then goes he to the length of all his arm,

And with his other hand thus o'er his brow

He falls to such perusal of my face

As a would draw it. Long stayed he so.

At last, a little shaking of mine arm,

And thrice his head thus waving up and down,

He raised a sigh so piteous and profound

That it did seem to shatter all his bulk

And end his being. That done, he lets me go,

And with his head over his shoulder turned,

He seemed to find his way without his eyes,

For out o'doors he went without their help,

And to the last bended their light on me.

Shakespeare Scenes

HAMLET ACT 3, SC 1

(Ophelia despairs at Hamlet's behaviour. Hamlet is much changed since the death of his father and is bent on revenge. Hamlet, is in a rage and angry against his mother and Ophelia. Hamlet has attacked Ophelia quite violently).

<u>Ophelia:</u>

O, what a noble mind is here o'erthrown!

The courtier's, soldier's scholar's eye, tongue, sword.

Th'expectancy and rose of the fair state,

The glass of fashion and the mold of form,

Th'observed of all observers, quite, quite, down!

And I, of ladies most deject and wretched,

That sucked the honey of his music vows,

Now see that noble and most sovereign reason

Like sweet bells jangled out of tune and harsh;

That unmatched form and feature of blown youth

Blasted with ecstasy. O woe is me,

T'have seen what I have seen, see what I see!

HAMLET ACT 4, SC 5

(Ophelia, distraught by the loss of her father and Hamlet's abusive treatment of her, has lost her mind. The verses in italics are sung. She is carrying flowers and herbs)

<u>Ophelia:</u>

Where is the beauteous majesty of Denmark?

How should I your true Love Know,

From another one?

By his cockle hat and staff

And his sandal shoon

(*Spoken*)

They say the owl was the baker's daughter. Lord we know what we are but not what we may be.

(*Sung*)

Tomorrow is Saint Valentine's Day

All in the morning betime

And I a maid at your window

To be your valentine

(*Spoken*)

I'll make an end on't

I hope all will be well. We must be patient; but I cannot choose but weep to think they would lay him in the cold ground.

There's rosemary, that for remembrance; pray you, love,

remember. And there's pansies, that's for thoughts. There's fennel for you, and columbines. There's rue for you, and here's some for me.

We may call it herb o' grace on Sundays. O, you must wear your rue with a difference. There's a daisy. I would give you some violets, but they withered all when my father died. They say a' made a good end.

(Sung).

He is dead and gone lady

He is dead and gone

By his head a grass green turf

At his head a stone

They bore him barefaced on the bier;

And in his grave rained many a tear.

Fare you well. My dove!

And will 'a not come again?

And will 'a not come again?

(Spoken)

No, no, he is dead,

He never will come again.

God 'a mercy on his soul

Shakespeare Scenes

CYMBELINE

Cymbeline is a tragedy but actually has a happy ending. The play is set in ancient Britain. King Cymbeline is on his second marriage and wishes for his daughter, Imogen to marry his new Queen's son. However, Imogen has secretly married her love, Posthumous. The new Queen is a wicked stepmother, just as in the fairy tales. She hates her step daughter and insists Posthumous is banished. Posthumous leaves for Italy where he meets the villainous, Iachimo. Iachimo bets that Imogen will be unfaithful to him. When he later visits England, he flirts with Imogen trying to persuade her to be unfaithful. However, Imogen is loyal to her husband and does not succumb to Iachimo's advances. Iachimo again tricks Imogen by hiding in a trunk in her bedchamber, noting all her belongings and stealing the bracelet given her by her husband. Cloten, the Queen's son continues to try to woo Imogen. Imogen realizes her bracelet is missing and is heartbroken. Iachimo by this time has returned to Rome and presents the bracelet as proof to Posthumous who is outraged. He sends a letter to his servant, Pisanio, to kill Imogen. Pisanio takes Imogen to Milford Haven under the pretence that he will meet Posthumous there. Meanwhile, close by in Wales, an old servant and courtier, named Belarius has been living in hiding and taking care of the King's long-lost sons. He stole them twenty years previously in revenge for having been banished by the King. Back in the forest, Pisanio, having lured Imogen to the forest, is unable to kill her despite the orders given by Posthumous. He helps Imogen dress as a young page in order to protect her identity and releases her. Meanwhile, back at the castle, Cloten, dresses in Posthumous's garments in order to find Imogen. Imogen is found in the forest by Belarius and the two young princes, little does she know they are in fact her brothers. As she is weary, Imogen drinks a potion she has been given not realising it is a sleeping potion which will feign her death. Cloten arrives in the forest and is captured and killed by one of Imogen's long-lost brothers. On returning to their cave, it appears as though Imogen is dead. They prepare a grave for her and leave. Not long after, Imogen awakens and is found by a Roman ambassador who has arrived to fight the English. He takes Imogen as his page. Meanwhile, a war breaks out between the Romans and the English. The two princes fight for Britain. Posthumous returns to fight for his country also. Posthumous is captured and imprisoned. He is eventually returned to the King who realizes the mistakes he has made. The Queen has died and he is happily reunited with his two sons. He forgives Belarius. He discovers that Imogen is the young page. Iachimo confesses his wrongdoings and Posthumous is happily reunited with his wife. Peace is declared with Rome.

CYMBELINE ACT 3 SCENE 4

(Imogen has been taken into the forest by her servant, Pisanio. Little does she know that Pisanio has been given orders to kill her by her husband, Posthumus)

<u>Imogen:</u>

Thou told'st me, when we came from horse, the place

Was near at hand: ne'er long'd my mother so

To see me first, as I have now. Pisanio! Man!

Where is Posthumus? What is in thy mind,

That makes thee stare thus? Wherefor breaks that sigh

From the inward of thee? One, but painted thus,

Would be interpreted a thing perplex'd

Beyond self- explication; put thyself

Into haviour of less fear, ere wildness

Vanquish my staider senses. What's the matter?

Why tender'st thou that paper to me with

A look untender? If 't be summer news,

Smile to 't before; if winterly, thou need'st

But keep that count'nance still. My husband's hand!

That drug- damn'd Italy hath out- crafted him,

And he's at some hard point. Speak, man; thy tongue

May take off some extremity, which to read

Would be even mortal to me.

(She reads the letter written by her husband, Posthumous)

Thy mistress, Pisanio, hath played the strumpet in

My bed; the testimonies whereof lie bleeding in me.

I speak not out of weak surmises, but from proof as

Strong as my grief and as certain as I expect my revenge.

That part thou, Pisanio, must act for me, if thy faith

Be not tainted with the breach of hers. Let thine own

Hands take away her life; I shall give thee opportunity

At Milford- Haven; she hath my letter for the purpose;

Where, if thou fear to strike, and to make me certain

It is done, thou art the pandar to her dishonour and

Equally to me disloyal.

False to his bed? What is it to be false?

To lie in watch there, and to think on him?

To weep 'twixt clock and clock? If sleep charge Nature,

To break it with a fearful dream of him,

And cry myself awake? That's false to's bed, is it?

HENRY VI PART 1

Henry VI is a trilogy and covers the War of the Roses. The young son of Henry V succeeds to the throne and becomes Henry VI, protected by Duke Humphrey. The English are still involved in battles in France. The French eventually win the battle against the English largely through the help of Joan of Arc, whom the English believe to be a sorceress. Joan of Arc is later burned at the stake. At home, there is a quarrel between the Lord Protector (Duke Humphrey) and the Cardinal of Winchester. There is civil unrest. Richard Plantagenet is made Duke of York. Richard Plantagenet is making claims to the crown and his followers wear white roses to represent the House of York and the House of Lancaster wear red roses. There are ongoing battles in different regions of France, but Henry craves peace. The earl of Suffolk has fallen in love with a beautiful, penniless Frenchwoman named Margaret of Anjou but as he is already married, offers her to the King instead. Henry marries Margaret but he is weak and Margaret is strong willed and is still in love with the Earl of Suffolk.

Shakespeare Scenes

HENRY 6TH (PART 1) ACT 1, SC 2

(Joan of Arc tells the Dauphin of her vision to help the French army claim victory against the English)

La Pucelle (Joan):

Where is the Dauphin? - Come, come from behind;

I know thee well, though never seen before.

Be not amaz'd, there is nothing hid from me:

In private will I talk with thee apart,

Stand back, you lords, and give us leave a while.

(Joan talks to the Dauphin alone).

Dauphin, I am by birth a shepherd's daughter,

My wit untrain'd in any kind of art.

Heaven and our Lady gracious hath it pleas'd

To shine on my contemptible estate:

Lo! Whilst I waited on my tender lambs,

And to sun's parching head display'd my cheeks,

God's mother deigned to appear to me;

And, in a vision full of majesty,

Will'd me to leave my based vocation,

And free my country from calamity.

Her aid she promis'd and assur'd success:

In complete glory she reveal'd herself;

And, whereas I was black and swart before,

With those clear rays, which she infus'd on me,

That beauty am I bless'd with, which you see.

Ask me what question thou canst possible,

And I will answer unpremeditated:

My courage try by combat, if thou dar'st,

And thou shalt find that I exceed my sex.

Resolve on this, - thou shalt be fortunate,

If thou receive me for thy warlike mate.

KING LEAR

King Lear is a tragedy. The 80 yr old King is becoming old and a little senile. It is time for him to relinquish his kingdom and share it between his three daughters, Gonerill, Regan and Cordelia. He states, in his foolishness, that whichever daughter proves to love him best will inherit most of his kingdom. As Cordelia is less sycophantic than her elder sisters, Lear childishly rejects his youngest daughter who had once been his favourite. Cordelia marries the King of France and leaves her two unscrupulous sisters to take care of their father. King Lear's prime minister, Gloucester is also betrayed by his son, Edmund, and his other faithful son, Edgar, is forced to go into hiding. The two sisters plot against their father and the king and his fool end up in the wilderness together, battling the elements. Gloucester, the prime minister, is blinded. The whole kingdom and the royal family collapse. The faithful Kent finds Lear and tries to protect him. It seems that his daughters do not care for him. In fact, Regan has been plotting against his life. Both daughters expel Lear from their homes. Lear manages to get to France where the French army, along with Cordelia, come to his rescue. By this time, Lear has gone quite mad. He makes his peace with the gentle Cordelia. There is a battle between the French and the English and the French are defeated. Lear and Cordelia are captured. Greedy for position, Goneril poisons her own sister, Regan. The evil Edmund is pronounced a traitor and the loyal Edgar wins the battle. Edgar orders Cordelia to be released but alas, it is too late. She has already been hanged. Lear enters with his daughter's dead body in his arms. King Lear dies of a broken hea

Shakespeare Scenes

KING LEAR ACT 4, SC 2

(Cordelia returns to visit her father, King Lear, to help him recover his throne)

Cordelia:

O you kind gods,

Cure this great breach in his abused nature;

The untuned and jarring senses, O, wind up

Of this child-changed father!

O my dear father, restoration hang

Thy medicine on my lips, and let this kiss

Repair those violent harms that my two sisters

Have in thy reverence made!

Had you not been their father, these white flakes

Did challenge pity of them. Was this a face

To be exposed against the warring winds,

To stand against the deep dread-bolted thunder,

In the most terrible and nimble stroke

Of quick cross-lightning, to watch – poor perdu –

With this thin helm? Mine enemy's dog,

Though he had bit me, should have stood that night

Against my fire. And wast thou fain, poor father,

To hovel thee with swine and rogues forlorn

In short and musty straw? Alack, alack,

'Tis wonder that thy life and wits at once

Had not concluded all! He wakes. Speak to him.

MACBETH

Macbeth is a tragedy with a theme of ambition. Macbeth and his wife end up destroying themselves by craving the throne of Scotland by any means possible. Macbeth and friend, Banquo, two great captains, are returning from battle and meet three witches on a heath who prophesy greatness. Duncan is the current king and bestows a new title on Macbeth for his loyalty and bravery. Macbeth is now Thane of Glamis and Cawdor. The witches have prophesied that he will be King and this has set Macbeth's ambition racing. He cannot wait to tell his wife, Lady Macbeth. He sends a letter to her, in advance of his return, informing her of his news. The witches have also prophesied that Banquo will have kings. King Duncan informs Macbeth that he will be visiting Macbeth's castle and Macbeth is tempted to murder him despite having some reservations. Lady Macbeth persuades her husband to kill Duncan while he is sleeping and blame the drunken guards. Macbeth is fearful and starts to visualise a bloody dagger before him. Lady Macbeth urges him to carry out the deed and assists him by smearing the king's blood over the guards. Shortly afterwards, Lord Macduff arrives at the castle and on visiting Duncan in his bed chamber finds him dead. Macbeth kills the two guards before the truth can be discovered. The king's sons escape to England in fear of their lives but some believe their exit proves them guilty. Macbeth is crowned King. He arranges to have Banquo and his son murdered. Banquo may have suspicions about Macbeth. Banquo shouts a warning to his son to escape. At supper that evening, the ghost of Banquo appears. Only Macbeth can see him and his guests notice his alarming behaviour. Macbeth seeks out the witches once again and he is told to beware Macduff and he should fear no one born of woman. A third apparition assures him of success until the time Birnam wood comes to Dunsinane. He is then faced with a line of kings with Banquo smiling on. Macbeth learns that Macduff has left for England to raise an army and Macbeth sends his murderers to kill

Lady Macduff and her sons. Lady Macbeth is haunted by her evil deeds and begins to sleepwalk. She ends up killing herself. Macduff has raised an army of English and Scottish soldiers and march upon Dunsinane. They disguise themselves as a marching forest. Macbeth's disloyal soldiers abandon him and surrender to the oncoming army. Macduff seeks out Macbeth and they fight. Macbeth is slain as Macduff was 'not of woman born' but born by caesarean. Malcolm is crowned King and peace is restored to Scotland.

MACBETH ACT 1, SC 3.

(three witches on a heath)

Witches:

Fair is foul, and foul is fair.

Hover through the fog and filthy air.

The weird sisters, hand in hand,

Posters of the sea and land,

Thus do go about, about:

Thrice to thine, and thrice to mine,

And thrice again, to make up nine.

Peace! The charm's wound up.

MACBETH, ACT 4, SC 1

(the witches make a spell)

Witch:

Round about the cauldron go;

In the poison'd entrails throw. –

Fillet of a fenny snake,

In the cauldron boile and bake;

Eye of newt, and toe of frog,

Wool of bat, and tongue of dog,

Adder's fork, and blind-worm's sting,

Lizard's leg, and howlet's wing,

For a charm of powerful trouble,

Like a hell-broth boil and bubble.

Double, double toil and trouble:

Fire, burn; and, cauldron, bubble.

MACBETH ACT 3, SC 5

(Hecate, the goddess of witchcraft, demands to know why she has been excluded from the witches meeting, regarding the fate of Macbeth)

Hecate:

Have I not reason, beldams as you are,

Saucy and overbold? How did you dare

To trade and traffic with Macbeth

In riddles and affairs of death;

And I, the mistress of your charms,

The close contriver of all harms

Was never call'd to bear my part,

Or show the glory of our art?

And, which is worse, all you have done

Hath been but for a wayward son,

Spiteful and wrathful, who, as others do,

Loves for his own ends, not for you.

But make amends now: get you gone,

And at the pit of Acheron

Meet me 'i the morning: thither he

Will come to know his destiny:

Your vessels and your spells provide,

Your charms and everything beside.

I am for the air; this night I'll spend

Unto a dismal and a fatal end:

Great business must be wrought ere noon.

Upon the corner of the moon

There hangs a vap'rous drop profound;

I'll catch it ere it come to ground:

And that distilled by magic sleights

Shall raise such artificial sprites

As by the strength of their illusion

Shall draw him on to his confusion.

He shall spurn fate, scorn death, and bear

His hopes 'bove wisdom, grace, and fear:

And you all know security

Is mortals' chiefest enemy.

Hark! I am called; my little spirit, see,

Sits in a foggy cloud and stays for me.

ROMEO AND JULIET

Believed to have been written between 1591 and 1595, Romeo and Juliet is a tragedy which is set in Verona, Italy. There is a feud between two houses: the house of Capulet and the house of Montague. Romeo does not join in the street-fighting between the two rival gangs. He is sick for the unrequited love of a young girl named Rosaline. Lord Capulet hosts a masked ball. He is keen for Paris to court his young daughter, Juliet. Romeo is dared by his friend, Benvolio, along with Mercutio, to gatecrash this ball. Romeo is easily persuaded as he believes that Rosaline will be there. On seeing Juliet, Romeo quickly forgets Rosaline. The fiery Capulet, Tybalt overhears Romeo asking after Juliet and realizes that he is a Montague. Romeo manages to dance with Juliet and steal a kiss from her. Juliet has now fallen in love with Romeo. That night, Romeo climbs the wall of the Capulet's house and finds Juliet on her balcony. They profess their love for each other and Romeo promises to find a way in which they can be married. Juliet arranges to send her beloved nurse the next morning at nine o'clock to finalize the arrangements. Romeo meets with the Friar who agrees to conduct a secret marriage. He hopes that marriage between two warring households may resolve matters. Tybalt has sent Romeo a letter challenging him to a duel. Romeo does not want to fight with Tybalt as he knows he is Juliet's cousin. Romeo and Juliet are secretly married that afternoon by Friar Laurence. The duel takes place and Mercutio is killed by Tybalt and despite Romeo's reluctance to fight, he is enraged at Mercutio's death and kills Tybalt. Romeo is banished and must leave Verona by the next morning and never return. Meanwhile, Juliet is waiting for Romeo to enjoy their wedding night. Her joy turns to sorrow when she learns from her nurse that Tybalt has been slain. Romeo spends the night with his new bride before leaving at dawn. That morning, Lady Capulet informs Juliet that she is to marry Paris. Juliet, in desperation, begs the Friar to help her. He offers her a potion which will feign the appearance of death. When she is laid in the vault, Romeo will be able to come and be reunited with her. Unfortunately, Romeo does not receive the letter and believes that Juliet is dead. Romeo buys poison so that he can lie alongside his beloved Juliet. Paris arrives at the tomb to mourn Juliet and sees Romeo. A duel ensues. Paris is killed. Romeo takes Juliet in his arms and drinks the poison. He kisses Juliet one last time. Juliet awakes to find Romeo dead. She then kills herself with a dagger no longer wishing to live. The violent feud between the two warring families is ended

ROMEO AND JULIET ACT 2, SC 5

(Juliet has met Romeo at a masked ball and has fallen in love with him. She has sent her Nurse to speak with him and is now impatiently awaiting her return)

<u>Juliet:</u> *(alone)*

The clock struck nine when I did send the Nurse.

In half an hour she promised to return.

Perchance she cannot meet him. That is not so.

O, she is lame! Love's heralds should be thoughts,

Which ten times faster glides than the suns beams

Driving back shadows over louring hills.

Therefore, do nimble-pinioned doves draw love,

And therefore, hath the wind swift Cupid wings.

Now the sun is upon the high most hill

Of this day's journey, and from nine till twelve

Is three long hours, yet she is not come.

Had she affections and warm youthful blood,

She would be as swift in motion as a ball.

Her words would bandy her to my sweet love,

And his to me.

But old folk, many feign as they were dead-

Unwieldy, slow, heavy and pale as lead.

(She sees her nurse coming, accompanied by Peter)

O God, she comes! O honey Nurse, what news?

Hast thou met with him? Send thy man away.

(The nurse sends Peter away).

Now, good sweet Nurse - O Lord, why lookest thou sad?

Though news be sad, yet tell them merrily.

If good, thou shamest the music of sweet news

By playing it to me with so sour a face.

(The nurse tells Juliet that her bones are aching).

I would thou hast my bones and I thy news.

Nay, come I pray thee speak. Good, Good Nurse, speak.

(The nurse tells Juliet that she is out of breath).

How art thou out of breath when thou hast breath

To say to me that thou art out of breath?

The excuse that thou dost make in this delay

Is longer than the tale thou dost excuse.

Is thy news good or bad? Answer to that.

Say either, and I'll stay the circumstance.

Let me be satisfied, is it good or bad?

No, no! But all this did I know before.

What says he of our marriage, what of that?

ROMEO & JULIET ACT 3, SC 2

(Juliet awaits Romeo to consummate their recent secret marriage. Little does she know that shortly her nurse will enter with some tragic news)

Juliet:

Gallop apace, you fiery-footed steeds,

Towards Phoebus' lodging! Such a waggoner

As Phaeton would whip you to the West

And bring in cloudy night immediately.

Spread thy close curtain, love-performing night,

That runaway's eyes may wink, and Romeo

Leap to these arms untalked of and unseen.

Lovers can see to do their amorous rites

By their own beauties; or, if love be blind,

It best agrees with night. Come, civil night,

Thou sober-suited matron, all in black,

And learn me how to lose a winning match,

Played for a pair of stainless maidenhoods.

Hood my unmanned blood, bating in my cheeks,

With thy black mantle till strange love grow bold,

Think true love acted simple modesty.

Come, night. Come, Romeo. Come, thou day in night;

For thou wilt lie upon the wings of night,

Whiter than new snow upon a raven's back.

Come, gentle night. Come, loving, black-browed night.

Give me my Romeo. And when I shall die,

Take him and cut him out in little stars,

And he will make the face of heaven so fine

That all the world will be in love with night

And pay no worship to the garish sun.

O I have bought the mansion of a love,

But not possessed it; and though I am sold,

Not yet enjoyed. So tedious is this day

As is the night before some festival

To an impatient child that hath new robes

And may not wear them.

O here comes my Nurse,

And she brings news; and every tongue that speaks

But Romeo's name speaks heavenly eloquence.

(The nurse enters)

Now, Nurse. What news?

ROMEO AND JULIET ACT 3, SC 2

(Juliet's nurse enters Juliet's bed chamber with the tragic news of her cousin, Tybalt's death)

<u>Juliet:</u>

      Blister'd be thy tongue

For such a wish! He was not born to shame.

Upon his brow shame is ashamed to sit;

For 'tis a throne where honor may be crown'd

Sole monarch of the universal earth.

O, what a beast was I to chide at him!

Shall I speak ill of him that is my husband?

Ah, poor my lord, what tongue shall smooth thy name

When I, thy three-hours wife, have mangled it?

But, wherefore, villain, didst thou kill my cousin?

That villain cousin would have killed my husband.

Back, foolish tears, back to your native spring;

Your tributary drops belong to woe,

Which you, mistaking, offer up to joy.

My husband lives, that Tybalt would have slain,

And Tybalt's dead, that would have slain my husband.

All this is comfort. Wherefore weep I then?

Some word there was, worser than Tybalt's death,

That murder'd me. I would forget it fain,

But, O, it presses to my memory

Like damned guilty deeds to sinners' minds:

"Tybalt is dead, and Romeo – banished".

That 'banished', that one word 'banished.'

Hath slain ten thousand Tybalts. Tybalt's death

Was woe enough, if it had ended there;

Or, if sour woe delights in fellowship

And needly will be rank'd with other griefs,

Why follow'd not, when she said "Tybalt's dead,"

'Thy father', or 'thy mother', nay, or both,

Which modern lamentation might have moved?

But with the rearward following Tybalt's death,

"Romeo is banished,'" to speak that word,

Is father, mother, Tybalt, Romeo, Juliet,

All slain, all dead. "Romeo is banished!"

There is no end, no limit, measure, bound,

In that word's death; no words can that woe sound.

O, find him! Give this ring to my true knight,

And bid him come to take his last farewell.

Shakespeare Scenes

ABOUT THE AUTHOR

Kim Gilbert trained as a professional actress at the Guildford School of Acting, studied for an LGSM with the Guildhall School of Music and Drama and took an English degree at the Open University. She has been acting, teaching and directing plays and musical productions for more than 35 years. She has experience in a wide range of theatre, TV and voiceover work. She has a First-class Honours degree in English and has taught English and Drama in many top schools in the country. Kim has examined for Lamda for a number of years and has also acted as an adjudicator. She has been running Dramatic Arts Studio for 11yrs, a private drama studio which specialises in developing excellence in all forms of performance and communication.

Shakespeare Scenes

Other Books by the same author:

<u>Shakespeare Scenes</u>

Monologues for young adult female actors

Duologues for female actors

Monologues for young male actors

<u>Chekhov Scenes</u>

Monologues & Duologues for women

<u>Scenes from Oscar Wilde</u>

Monologues & Duologues for female actors

Monologues for Male actors

Duologues from Oscar Wilde

<u>Classic Monologues for female actors</u>

<u>Improve Your Voice</u>

How to speak English with confidence

Available from Amazon Bookstore

"Thankyou for reading! If you enjoyed this book or found it useful, I'd be very grateful if you'd post a short review on Amazon. Your support really does make a difference and I read all the reviews personally so I can get your feedback and make this book even better. Thanks again for your support!"

Shakespeare Scenes

Shakespeare Scenes

Printed in Great Britain
by Amazon